Illustrations by Joan Thoubboron

Copyright © 1998, 1999, 2001 Modern Publishing, a division of Unisystems, Inc.
Previously published as ™Fun-To-Read Fairy Tales.
All rights reserved.
® Honey Bear Books is a trademark owned by Honey Bear Productions, Inc.,
and is registered in the U.S. Patent and Trademark Office. No part of this book may be
reproduced or copied without written permission from the publisher.
All rights reserved. Printed in China.

CHRISTMAS CLASSICS
The Night Before Christmas

MODERN PUBLISHING
A Division of Unisystems, Inc.
New York, New York 10022
Series UPC Number: 39495

'Twas the night before Christmas,
    when all through the house
Not a creature was stirring,
    not even a mouse;
The stockings were hung
    by the chimney with care,
In hopes that St. Nicholas
    soon would be there.

The children were nestled
all snug in their beds,
While visions of sugar-plums
danced in their heads.

And Mama in her kerchief,
and I in my cap,
Had just settled our brains
for a long winter's nap,
When out on the lawn there
arose such a clatter,

I sprang from my bed to see
    what was the matter.
Away to the window
    I flew like a flash,
Tore open the shutters
    and threw up the sash.

The moon on the breast
   of the new-fallen snow
Gave a luster of midday
   to objects below;
When what to my wondering
   eyes should appear,
But a miniature sleigh
   and eight tiny reindeer,
With a little old driver,
   so lively and quick,
I knew in a moment
   it must be St. Nick.

More rapid than eagles
  his coursers they came,
And he whistled and shouted,
  and called them by name:
"Now Dasher! Now, Dancer!
  Now, Prancer and Vixen!
On, Comet! On, Cupid!
  On, Donder and Blitzen!
To the top of the porch,
  to the top of the wall!
Now dash away, dash away,
  dash away, all!"

As dry leaves that before
   the wild hurricane fly,
When they meet with an obstacle,
   mount to the sky,
So up to the housetop
   the coursers they flew,
With the sleigh full of toys,
   and St. Nicholas too.

And then in a twinkling
   I heard on the roof
The prancing and pawing
   of each little hoof.
As I drew in my head,
   and was turning around,
Down the chimney St. Nicholas
   came with a bound.

He was dressed all in fur,
    from his head to his foot,
And his clothes were all tarnished
    with ashes and soot.
A bundle of toys he had
    flung on his back,
And he looked like a peddler
    just opening his pack.

His eyes how they twinkled,
   his dimples how merry!
His cheeks were like roses,
   his nose like a cherry!
His droll little mouth
   was drawn up like a bow,
And the beard on his chin
   was as white as the snow;
The stump of his pipe
   he held tight in his teeth,
And the smoke it encircled
   his head like a wreath;
He had a broad face
   and a little round belly
That shook, when he laughed,
   like a bowl full of jelly.

He was chubby and plump,
   a right jolly old elf,
And I laughed when I saw him,
   in spite of myself;
A wink of his eye and
   a twist of his head,
Soon gave me to know
   I had nothing to dread.

He spoke not a word, but
went straight to his work,
And he filled all the stockings;
then turned with a jerk,

And laying his finger aside of his nose,
And giving a nod, up the chimney he rose.

He sprang to his sleigh,
    to his team gave a whistle,
And away they all flew
    like the down of a thistle.

But I heard him exclaim,
   ere he drove out of sight,
"Happy Christmas to all,
   and to all a good night!"